Democracy In Chains

Songs For A Wailing World

By

George O. Obikoya

Book 1

Yesterday heralds tomorrow not today, a day erased we cannot regain straddling a space, agape its portal to the waves we strive to figure here in vain, not those we chorus daily not our everyday air atmospheric laid, yet we are wont to keep our fate with destiny we are unsure will fail, faltering not in our lexicon let alone failing we quietly affirm resolved to fix our face, our precious void O yea, we are certain we will, even without a day we'll rather wish away, no matter hard we strive to comprehend the link between the past and the future of our voided space, perhaps knowing all those panopticons are everywhere, even in our sanctuary, perhaps knowing Foucault is saying 'I told you so,' wherever he is now, perhaps realizing everybody is indeed deceased, well, almond-eyed watchers, everyone or whatever busy eyeing everyone whenever wherever re-educating our void.

O yes, with lies big and small cremating care: did someone say lies voiding empathy, or is it straddling its hiatus re-defining it? Lord have mercy! It is unlikely anyone would disagree that lies are the antithesis of goodness, put differently, lying is evil and, by extension, liars, so what would persons who embrace liars be, those who vote herein for politicians who peddle lies, for example, what would they be? The glue that binds society and is the bedrock of civilization is morality, the alternative dear mates is Hobbesian, right? So folks, why do we pretend we reform when we exploit, contract services contractors may profit from the sweat of the condemned we claim to thereby reform, in effect, an institutional lie, panopticons everywhere to be sure we 'behave'? You see, folks, liars the reformers! That's the stuff that day is made of that does not exist, the day of the vibrations.

Indeed, vibrations or waves peculiar in the realm that was all good in the aeons and could still be, O yes, couldn't it folks? Ask Enki, not Enlil, as we struggle to find the answer to that intriguing question peddling and embracing lies, of course our every move eyed in void by bizarre orbs posing as eyes that grade us on a social scale pretty much as they do yea on a credit scale, you know, liars the graders, the pervasive inversion that's the stuff that day is made of we want to wish away rather than work to change, after all, we only need to wave our magic wand and puff, it's gone away hidden here in our pates in layers of meaning that straddle tomorrow and yesterday drowning, our civilization in a deluge of lies herein in misinformation declared truths miasmic waves dispense dispersed vibrations contaminating primal waves pervasive in a voided space we call abode, our precious world, by a fly, of sorts.

So, the vibrations manifest in phenomena are flawed relative to the noumena, the essence, courtesy of contaminating vibrations that make our day appear non-existent, wished away, or so we hoped whereas we live them everyday, as if nothing is amiss: there is nothing to worry about let them straddle the void we create living day by day not as if unperturbed but as if we are helpless against the formidable vibrations we all create, pardon me, or as may be the case, someone made us create, or someone created yea on our behalf, signed up after all with this creator here O yea, you know, something like that: vibrations self-made, or contractor-made ravaging our voided space unfazed while we stand aside and let it all happen as long as we have our rice and razzmatazz, right? Who wants to risk all that trying to solve the world's problems? No one really: there is no problem to solve, today does not exist, yesterday, gone.

Tomorrow? We've got it figured out, no worries, it's going to be just more of today, O yes!
Relax! It's all good. Yeah right! Isn't it? Never mind who hid that owl on the dollar bill, forget
about those eyes everywhere, or the 'holdouts' in the upper house never mind who the billionaires
are who don't want to pay taxes or prefer paying pittance, forget all the 'civics' you ever
learnt in school, that was yesterday, this is today says the 'wise one,' it's a brand new day! You need to
imbibe all the Lethe available wherever, just get drunk, okay, stop stressing yourself mates
thinking about undergoing psychological testing for MCI, you do not have 'mild
cognitive impairment' you are just Lethe-drunk! Good for you, at least you only have to worry
about cleaning out your gut for the next round of ten bowls of rice and twenty crispy fried turkey
drumsticks for dinner: poor thing, that's the bottom line, right? Another Nero incarnate, ah, ah, ah.

By the way, aren't we not supposed to talk about that! Aren't we meant to be aporetic,
silent, don't complain don't explain, just calculate, Mr. Bohr? Pardon me, can we now talk about
embodied and disembodied spirits? Thank goodness yesterday is gone, or is today the 'dark
ages' back again, everyone, dead, motorized carrions, right? Right. Lord have mercy! Do you see
why we ask all those 'quixotic' questions as some put them? For Pete's sake who would herein not wonder
what a moth is doing in their glass of water hours after talking about moths and rice? Never
mind, it's just a moth committing hara-kiri in plain sight seeking the light! What the heck? Cool it
down mate, don't freak out over a dead moth, it's all vicariousness, right? Okay, I'm good! Well, in
a manner of speaking, opened up new learning enterprises in novel vistas regarding
those miasmic 'disembodied' vibrations thing, or are they embodied? Yes! Seriously?

Let's just say they may or may not be embodied! So, today is disconnected from the past and
the future as we deem it being embodied or disembodied waves herein in a void, and we
are all responsible one way or another for goings on in a voided space we all call
our home wherein, as Foucault noted, power is everywhere with which folks we agree, yes, today
is unlike where the 'hollow men' reside where there are no eyes, and TS Eliot would probably
agree as well: there are orbs everywhere here folks, even in our sanctuaries O yea, eyes are
us! And their portals, ley lands are everywhere wherein vibrations pop and puff in the weird abyss
of today that blends into the memories of yesterday and the hopes of tomorrow we seek,
right, folks? We conveniently erase today so it does not contaminate tomorrow right?
Which suggests we want tomorrow to be better than today, or maybe we're just thrill-seekers!

Yes, adventurers in an imagined infinite-dimensional space, well, Hilbert space if you
like, the future endlessly endless sort of, so, why spoil it? You know, matters might be different
were some 'brane' going to wallop it anyways, right? Which may, dear mates perhaps explain the seeming
nonchalance attitude folks have towards climate change, for instance, which may be an aspect of the
pervasive cremation of care herein in a void why would anyone care about a finite
void? So, let there be even more eyes after all why wouldn't Plato say the Absolute is not
infinite: the more the eyes surveilling the caves the easier it would be to get us all figured
out, ensure we play only for today, yes, forget about tomorrow, in other words, we want
yea to erase today not because we care about tomorrow, even a better tomorrow
but because we don't: there's no tomorrow not to mention an infinite one, none whatsoever.

Whereas the intergalactic music of the spheres emanates we believe in an infinite
inter-dimensional non-spherical realm hence we have not much to say about its attributes

in the language of its songs in a spherical realm wherein our void resides, we still must air the
air of infinitude in situ finite laid, we still must not straddle void we must dear folks bridge
tomorrow and the days afore, the days of yore we must not discount as they may explain what we
really think about the future and what it may or may not bring today portends, so let's see what
we may do to modify goings on in our void today for the better and not continue
to play 'ostrich' yea, for we don't want to be Nero we want to be who we really are, except
we are indeed, reincarnated, in any case, matters may just end very badly as they
did for the fellow, and we don't want that, or do we? Let's just say we don't, regardless of our waves!

Seeing what those virulent vibrations are doing to us all seeing the pain they are spreading
here in a void who in their right mind would not want these to stop, after all, they still love the rice and
razzmatazz, right? They don't want to lose the yachts they want to take the limo across the Acheron
yes possibly even that craft you could float in upside down touring outer space, poor Charon, what
now, your canoe might capsize? In the days people are herein talking about the variants and
sub-variants of viruses we cannot afford to ignore the songs we sing today, and the
mathematical algorithms we devise dear mates to implicate the Absolute in some
'reflection principle' thing! Lord have mercy! We must take responsibility for messing up our
world, the essence, the One, we cannot characterize with an intergalactic tongue, no we can't,
the best we can do is speculate, we can't be sure it has this or that attributes, not at all.

Book 2

Why wouldn't we want to be held accountable for our actions, why should anyone persist in denial of the damage we are doing to our very precious world? Perhaps we should ask more pointedly: what really killed Georg Cantor what gave him that heart attack in a pink house, is it the 'bipolar disorder' he allegedly had or the relentless criticism by his so-called colleagues of the so-called 'dangerous knowledge' he had regarding infinity who killed the man? Folks: leave that! No, we won't, because to kill 'dangerous knowledge' is still a notion widely held in our voided space, an extension of the shameless denial of responsibility we earlier talked about, complete with the persecution, even killing of the likes of Georg yea herein here and now, witness the wanton kidnapping, incarcerating without due process and the butchering of journalists worldwide, folks academics are being denied grants for doing 'wrong.'

Doing 'wrong' is doing the 'wrong' research, which is a 'crime' for which you must be hunted down by your 'right' meta-narrative-peddling professors as they did to Georg O yes: talk about how Popper might have felt about Kuhn, but 'paradigm shift' is alive and well, Georg's ideas are alive and well, so are those of the slain journalists, O yes dear mates, so are the ideas of Socrates, Copernicus, Spinoza, Giordano Bruno, Galileo, Cantor and many other 'trail-blazers of thought': they live on herein dear mates, they live on. You can kill whoever but you can't kill their ideas, talk about Nag Hammadi, talk about the Dead Sea scrolls, ideas live on, way past tomorrow no matter how hard you try to kill them today, O yes, way past the 'Shylocks' of the day, the so-called moneybags purveyors and patrons of meta-narratives yea, way past these nutters and their 'bags,' so folks we must expose the sword-less fiends lurking herein in our void, yes.

We don't need to be afraid of waves after all we are all partakers in the music of the spheres embedded in an inter-dimensional realm to which a primal spark herein connects yea materialized in everyone of us, as such, a spark whose intensity varies with its strength which itself varies and our actions herein determines yea, brighter if we lived in the light and darker if we lived in darkness: makes sense, right? In other words O mates, we all determine yes how strong our yoke with ane is depending on whether we live a life of goodness and virtue or an evil life, that being simply it why must we be afraid folks, afraid of what? What are we so we must goad ourselves to hell, as some traditions term where evil people go after death, what folks? What is that makes us want to keep doing evil and think we can get away with it when we are embedded within an infinite inter-dimensional realm, within alpha and omega?

Perhaps we could say that thing might also be assuring us dear mates that there is no such thing as the afterlife, who knows? So, who cares about tomorrow, we may conclude and live our lives as if there's none. We may not care about climate change and global warming because 'in entropy we trust,' and we care nothing about yesterday because it's dead and gone, yet we care about rice and yes razzmatazz because we are 'frogging' alive and well and we want to prove it! We want to wear our designer clothes and calico shoes and show off our new cottages at the lake, yes we want our family, neighbours and friends to see how well off we are; did we forget anyone? O yes, let's add our dog to the list and like Caligula, our horse, yes it could rival Incitatus, right? Lord have mercy, we could add our cats we could include our daffodils to blare their tubas while we chorus atop the hill with like-minded phenomena float away from the spark within, herein.

Is that all? Is life a gong show? Maybe, if you asked a fop! But we are not all dandies are we?
Certainly not, some of are, many are not, so are we going to let fops turn us all into
fops, educated naughts? We think not although we may be wrong; we hope not, for so much is at stake
our world we must defend and protect from ghouls, and gravediggers yea, some of these felons used to dig
tunnels to reach corpses to steal and sell, corpses buried much deeper than six feet, to prevent them
being stolen and sold, in the first place, to anatomists who used them to teach medical students:
these days those panopticons ensure there enough homeless folks for the anatomists' cadavers
down the road! What a difference today makes folks, what a big difference one single day makes to
yesterday and, by the way, that these crooks stole and still steal valuables such as jewelry used
by the wealthy to adorn their deceased relatives shows some things don't change: evil, ever evil?

Okay, life is a gong show but who or what are the key players, beings from outer space yes as the
Sumerians claimed, toying with primitive humans' genes and fighting one another herein in
a void, is that it, no God involved, nothing just 'the powerful ones,' 'sky people,' 'Elohim' and
us as we were in the days of yore or are these Anunnaki still here doing the exact same
things they were doing thousands of years ago, fighting over control of void? By the way, what were
they fighting to gain control of? Territory or humans and why? If they were still here, is there
agenda the same and why is it taking so long to achieve their aims if they were so potent
and could, and will tomorrow change the status quo or will things forever remain the same herein?
Some would argue something or another is here able to instil fear in folks, intimidate
them, this thing somehow miasmic able to take control of their minds wherever they are in our world.

Just thinking about that is scary folks, isn't it? Yet can we thumb our chests and declare this is
impossible? Probably not, as weird as it all seem, after all we have seen folks invading
parliaments on the orders of some 'boss,' beheading people, chopping them into bits and yes
incinerating them on such orders, we have seen these zombified actions and wonder what the
heck happened to our folks who made them zombies and why? Maybe these 'potent' entities are still here
playing their game organizing their gong shows folks in a voided space? Perhaps we'll find answers
to these queries exploring miasmic waves! We may find out waves are us, and them, yes, we may find
out we are all vibrations in an intergalactic realm materialized, which may explain
why these potent ones sometimes crash their crafts near military installations, you know and are yea
reportedly captured albeit half-alive and nurtured back to life: one wonders if they drank milk!

Yes if they favoured roast beef sandwich over chicken sandwich indeed, if they washed down their meals in
here with some choice red wine, or lager must also be on our minds, after all we are all spirits,
mattered or not, herein in a void, many of us in denial about today wishing it
does not exist, preferring to live it to the fullest with our rice and razzmatazz not worried
about tomorrow which does not exist in the minds of some of us anyways, even when it's
not yet past midnight in our location, you know, so what? We hear some say that not surprisingly,
after all they also declare elections rigged before votes are cast, that is only if they lost though,
bizarre eh? Let there be darkness they must chorus in their coves admonishing an owl for smashing
their asses again with a hot iron rod, perhaps for not cremating care enough, or maybe
for not caring for folks enough to not grant them freedom to choose who to vote for, enough, O yea.

O dear, you ought to stifle them the wise one responded in defence you ought render them poor and
ineffective that's what is right: yea yea yea all present replied in unison we hear you loud

and clear, perhaps saying to please the bird, so you, the bird is not claiming to be all that potent,
nor are the folks subordinate to it, or so it seems, after all waves are us as they are dear
mates, a bird, be it a raven or an owl and, by the way, we do not suppose an erectile
reptile or a bipedal humanoid ant would claim it is, which makes the ash smashing more germane
than the ass itself in the greater scheme which perhaps explains why folks complained about it to the
owl, in other words, in exploring our void for answers to the questions we asked, we are looking
for actions not form, we are looking not for 'cat eyes' or 'lizard eyes,' whose waves might yes be fleeting
artful dodgers anyway, but for what these entities parasitizing in folks are doing.

Or, better still, what they are making folks do: this distinction is key in figuring who or what
really does not want today to exist and straddling yesterday and tomorrow and why. It is
not only a heuristic but also a pragmatic distinction to make. It affords us all
a chance to see the inner workings of the variety of 'sub-variants' of the music of
the spheres elements of which we all in terms of the waves constituting us, waves accruing yea
over time upon our primal framework of waves, that atavistic spark that links us with the One
to a more or less extent depending on the nature of the vibrations comprising herein
its epigenetic epiphenomena, put differently, whether we have been living
in darkness or light, which is instructive indeed folks and is a solid basis for whatever
action we choose to take regarding defending and protecting our void against bugs, for instance.

Book 3

Yes, indeed folks, vibrations may manifest as viruses and bugs as they may in queens and kings, and we know what these manifestations of vibrations did through history, and what the high priests also did and continue to do, we are witnesses to their ideological, doctrinal and other effusions of versions of the 'truth' that mesmerize the tots regarding void, the one to straddle and the one to toss, today. So, we have waves manifesting one way or another, but could they manifest as different things at once, you know, one moment as a human, the next as a virus, a bug or a parasite? In other words could the virus and it variants and sub-variants yea wreaking havoc in void be some humans transformed? Seriously? You've got to be kidding! No mate, not really after all some folks are said to be capable of 'remote viewing,' right? Some folks have conversations with their plants and since quantum tunnelling does not seem that spooky after all O yes.

No it's not, now that we have all been converted, at least since the mid-C20th, to the doctrine known as Heisenberg Uncertainty Principle and can see how quantum tunnelling enables objects, which can be waves or particles, penetrate the barriers of classical mechanics, such as a solid wall, 'unscathed,' energy wise that is, and quantum computing is enabling quantum information systems at unbelievably speeds folks that the 'error correction' that plagues quantum states needed for such issues as quantum decoherence, the loss of the required phase relationships between quantum states for quantum computing to 'work,' once adequately addressed, may dear mates here empower adherents of the Everettian school taunt those of the Copenhagen school of quantum mechanics regarding the veracity of the latter's assumed probabilistic bent of wavefunction which still picks 'favoured' configurations.

Indeed, waves may here have 'favoured' configurations according to the former school which, in the final analysis implies a deterministic manner of probabilistic waves, which suggests that the resolution of the 'error correction' issue may make quantum computing more generally applicable in the real world, better than classical computing, if not in computability, in speed, whether that is a good thing or not, we'll wait and see, or should we? Do we want to see all of us having conversations with plants, ants and lizards, more so in a deterministic manner? In other words, the nature of the conversations dependent on the sway held by the constituent conversant, who may choose to toss today yes, with all the ramifications of such a choice, this dominant conversant, perhaps a plant or a lizard! Things may already be heading in this direction herein with the push of big tech towards 'sway.'

Yes, folks towards a 'virtual reality' accessible to everyone who could utilize whatever means to access the 'cave,' a 'virtual reality' wherein dominant waves can potentially deluge with miasmic grand narratives in quantum-tunnelling waves! Please Lord have mercy! Aren't we already seeing that on social media? Now, it is going to be tunnelled straight into our pates dear mates. You see, the notion of a deterministic wavefunction assumes the favoured configuration is the most 'popular,' commonest configuration, in other words, determined by numbers, so, in saying a small group of ants or lizards are now going to hold sway and determine the favoured configuration are we saying numbers don't count anymore, you know, that democracy no longer matters, or are we thinking this small group may 'buy' folks herein with their wherewithal, monetarily or via lies and misinformation.

Are we saying they will buy the numbers and have their way at the polls? Now, this is not a joking
matter, not at all, it is something we ought to seriously mull and prevent! We must not sit
back and let some ridiculous straddling take over our notions of the arrow of time just so
we are coerced into living in the darkness of Platonic caves chasing shadows yea: we must
not do that folks we must not mortgage our future and that of our children and grandchildren, that of
all those coming after us. Folks we must be honest and admit we cannot rule out the above
scenarios no matter how much we want to toss today, we must consider the prospects of
'aliens' living here among us, 'aliens,' indeed when they are just configurations much
like the rest of us roaming an intergalactic realm, something we must ponder, no matter how
uncomfortable it makes us feel, if we really wanted to comprehend goings on in void.

It may be hard to see things this way after all, we have been brought up to see them in other ways,
we have been configured, so to speak, to the world in the classical-mechanics way, not as waves
that become particles when measured or shall we say, seen, in other words, we don't see waves we see
a spouse, we don't see waves we see a sibling we don't see waves we see a dog, a plant and the chair
we are about to sit on, our world is concrete not intangible, it is tangible, so, why
should anyone expect us to suddenly start to see waves rather these solid tangible folks
and things, this reality we are familiar with? Yet, we must beat big tech and co to it,
we must adapt to thinking about virtual reality and the world of waves, lest folks it
swallows us like our current notions of goings on in the world have enslaved us: we cannot at
all afford to be permanently enslaved folks it's time we freed ourselves from bondage in a cave.

O yes it is, we must not ignore the writings on the wall and let our enslavement continue,
no we must not, we must not be demoralized by the Leviathan nor must we throw our hands
up in the air and surrender to viruses no matter the variant or sub-variant
yea, we need to remember the variety of wavefunction that may be operational
herein and their prospects of becoming deterministic from being probabilistic yes once
materialized and configured as determined by the dominant or favoured waves as our
analysis has so far shown, and we appreciate the fact that what we are saying may sound
like jargon to some folks but we cannot and must not ignore, dear mates, where our analysis sought
eclectically in science, religion, politics, philosophy, law and mythology
among others, leads, no matter how speculative or, as some folks might even argue, weird yea.

True, they may seem strange or quixotic to some folks but we must not ignore our analysis, more
so given the importance of the knowledge we seek, knowledge of the forces here in void dear mates
determining our fate, as it seems, you know, whether or not we ought to have any knowledge at
all and if so, how much, as some traditions say, that we may not become gods like them, so, is it
unreasonable to seek knowledge of these gods who, being gods, might be privy to what is herein
happening to us today we must not remember, gods that might know a thing or two about the
virus now ravaging void throwing our world into chaos, you know, these gods that might be morphing
into one thing or another including bugs, gods that seem to want to keep us perpetually
in chains in Platonic caves chasing shadows yes, is there anything wrong with seeking to know just
a little something about these gods, who some traditions refer to as the 'Elohim,' O yes?

The so-called 'powerful ones,' we must explore we need to know about before we're all 'deceased' in
the hands of bugs, and we put deceased in parenthesis because we do not think these gods would want

to kill all their slaves, maybe they just don't need as many they now have in their hands and need to kill
a few of us, who knows what happened to their dietary habits? Lord have mercy! So, folks we
must get serious and face the face we need to face and be not afraid, there is no time to waste,
the virus is morphing playing Houdini messing with our pates, why must we be silent and yes
acquiesce to this nonsense dear mates, is it because of rice and razzmatazz? Do we want to
keep being slaves when we have the opportunity to break free of the fangs of snakes? Let's be honest,
we are all slaves no matter how many private jets we own if still groping in Platonic caves.
We are servants of ants, lizards, viruses or whatever these demonic waves morph into yes.

Truth may indeed, be bitter and uncomfortable but we must not deny it because of how
we feel, we must face and address it, not cringe and retreat into our closets to curl up therein
in a foetal position trembling like a leaf blown hither and yon hiding from ourselves, yes, for
who or what we are hiding from must already be parasitizing on us instilling fear
in us is why we are so afraid: folks remember that, 'we have nothing to fear but fear itself'
a respected elder statesman once declared, and rightly so, let's not be afraid to call a spade
a spade, call out those among us morphing into bugs creating chaos in our precious world, let
us all go out there and vote them out or never vote them into office on Election Day, we
must let them know we have had enough of their antics and want out, they must know we need our today
and no one is going to bully-straddle it to feed their lunatic whims enough is enough!

Book 4

Folks, we must be determined to be free: our freedom is not negotiable. We want
nothing less than being free. So, we want to be free, from bugs, from viruses, or waves? Verily we
believe we were all born free and reclaim that freedom here and now, today. So, folks no straddling in
our days is allowed, none at all, we don't want to forget today we want to own and remember
it, right folks? We realize we are talking about waves, about frequencies, vibrations, ghosts.
spirits, consciousnesses, take your pick, we are talking dear mates about some probabilistic-turned-
deterministic wavefunction tweaking void in keeping with agenda which is intriguing
and makes us want to play archeologists for a while, excavate the truth regarding our world,
our mysterious void, the truth many folks may find uncomfortable to accept, we want to
dig deep into the minds of folks to better understand our world, a worthy exercise indeed.

You see, the notion that someone, or something, the physical manifestation of waves wants
us to assume today does not exist is itself suggestive yea of a diabolical
hidden agenda on their part, since they are not saying why they want today erased. On the
other hand they may simply don't dear mates believe in today being different from yesterday and
tomorrow yea, you know, preferring to believe in only the here and now, which does not need to
be remembered because there is no tomorrow anyway and yesterday also did not in
in exist since it was configured for consciousnesses no longer in existence, in effect
emphasizing the continuously changing nature of wavefunction herein in our voided
space in a deterministic manner manifest, as such, time itself does not exist since it
is different for every new configuration of waves manifest herein in a void, yes.

So, in this perspective, waves are ephemeral as they change all the time, the experiences
we have only determined to the extent that we must have them being still materially here
manifest. Perhaps this explains the notion of straddling wherein yesterday and tomorrow are
merged into an ever-changing today one moment of which is dear mates necessarily
a different wavefunction collapse than the next and as such we must forget. Folks, this may be the
'logic' behind the notion of straddling some waves, or consciousnesses seem to peddle in a void
and use to justify the atrocities they carry out in our precious world, who knows, mates, who
does? By the way, should we, therefore, find the debaucheries and revelries our so-called leaders yea
engage in camped in the woods annually for weeks, starting folks with the incineration of
a human effigy, or is it a child as some claim, surprising? Are they fiends in government?

Leaders, not only in government but also in academia, industry and indeed,
all spheres of life from all over the world, thousands of them invited to partake yes in drunken
revelries, engage in rituals and pee all over the place under the watchful eyes of an
owl, their own panopticon that ensures they cremate care! So, why would such waves not want to forget
their peeing frenzy when they return to their spherical offices? You see folks, we all ought to
be tired of the antics of these dementing waves locked here in some Sumerian past: enough is
enough! These waves or what they see as gods and worship are all just intergalactic waves like the
rest of us they empower in demonic configurations forming insane alliances
deep in the woods in some remote locations in the dark! So, are these waves privy to goings on
in our void such as the havoc a virus has been wreaking on us all for several months now?

Are they, really and truly? Wow! Ok, we may want to ask the Ethiopians why they are
seven years behind the rest of other Africans or why, unlike their West African counterparts who
dance with their hips, they dance with their shoulders folks in what they call 'Eskistas,' the interpretation
of which is 'dancing shoulders,' in case this notion of time being different for everyone is yes
somehow confusing, you know: let's even leave Einstein's special relativity theory out
of the discussion. Yet, we need to take a closer look at the interpretation some people
in our midst have given this notion in their bid to perpetuate their hidden agendas here
in void, what appears to be the permanent enslavement of the human race carried out using
a variety of tactics to manipulate waves, to ensure the determination of
wavefunction's 'determining' potential regarding goings on in void, telling us we are fried!

That is what all their shenanigans amount to folks, that they determine our fate and they say there's
absolutely nothing we can do about it! Lord have mercy! Yes, there are the Knights of this and
that, Knights of Timbuktu, the Brotherhood of the Owl, the Sorority of the Angels and yes
whatever, all waiting for you! So, behave! What? Don't even think about it. We've got you fools all
figured out, okay, so behave. Yes, a conversation of some waves may go like that in Phantom
Farms, abode of animals and the ghouls who want to steal us 'dead or alive,' after all, Cromwell
was exhumed and impaled for everyone to see and smell his rotten corpse, well, to serve herein as
a deterrent to anyone contemplating beheading a monk, regardless in white or black
soutane! Lord have mercy! What the heck is going on here? Well, you better believe it dear mates, it's
a global gong show! Yes, I agree in toto, orchestrated by some inebriated louts.

What is going on may be some pee-loving dementing waves and their soulmates goading us to hell
where they are from and we must send them back to, pronto. Remember, they affirm they have all of us
figured out which may be a metaphor yes for 'dumbed down,' who knows? Probably, they have herein paid
'remote viewers' and psychics working in those ubiquitous panopticons so they know when you
are peeing or trying to be funny showing signs of 'too know,' and don't forget, those Club of Gog
'initiates' are waiting for you in Magog, so, behave! By the way, why do these so-called all-
powerful gods still ask their comrade-in-arms where they are going when just about to die, shouldn't
they already know they are going to hell? Maybe they are hoping yes to somehow chicane to
Eden's gate, you know, bribe Charon. What we take away from this is that they are not all-powerful
at all: they are concerned about where they head in 'afterlife,' which means they believe in 'afterlife.'

They believe in the afterlife and have no clue where exactly they are going perhaps not that
oblivious to the repercussions of their evil deeds while alive. Also, they are simply
intergalactic waves like the rest of us, only coated in embroidered soutanes in fish-head
gears sitting on gold-rimmed stools or whatever bamboozling all of us here with meta-virtual
reality gobbledegook herein in a voided space to perpetuate folks, their insane
agendas incinerating tots to please, ostensibly, some god, some spider, ant or snake, some
whatever yea: is this sort of craziness what should ever be happening, more so in this day
and age? Yeah, we are not supposed to ask any questions about it, right? Ask questions and you are
a goner, every lizard down the 'externalized' hierarchy unleashed upon you up in arms
ready to cannibalize your pate; O what a sorry state, one we must elect to change for good.

We must make our world a better place for everyone of us, O yea. We must no longer sit on
the fence playing ostrich folks: we must not pretend we are inoculated against the ills of

society and the conspiracy of some waves to keep all enslaved, we must call out these clowns,
these obnoxious drag kings and queens, rum-loving malicious waves and hold them accountable for
their evilness toward humanity. Not only must we not let them get away with what they
have done creating chaos fomenting trouble in the world, but we must also stop them dear mates
perpetuating these ills and keeping us all chained down in Platonic caves: we must set ourselves
and our world free, folks, once and for all. So, we must continue to have them figured out, yes, they say
they have us all figured out, we tell them we have them even more figured out than their dementing
pates can ever tell, and we are learning more about them faster than 'the speed of light,' almost so.

The 'thing' is that they all fear and expect us all to fear even more we care no hoot about: we
are not encased like mummies in some Sumerian sarcophagus? We are not beholden to
some tot-wolfing owl or whatever and we have no tophets to hide, so in effect we are in
fact already free, you know, our minds have been liberated in the light of higher waves, why we
are not intimidated by their ugly policies of encirclement or whatever yea.
Folks, we are determined to continue to work hard to stay free and break the chains of slavery
they have our folks who have not seen the light in, our captured, zombified folks languishing in mental
gaols and we will free them, so mote it be, we will all be free of oppression, we will break free of
victimization in the hands of waves morphing into viruses here or from beyond as some
of them used to threaten us they would, you know, return here after death as viruses to kill.

Book 5

Indeed folks, who knows if these waves are now fulfilling their promise to return here from the grave as
viruses to kill many of us and trim down the human population which they deemed too high?
Who knows? One key issue to bear in mind is that our woes are traceable to us, to some of us
here with agendas that are harmful to the rest of us, but whose agendas are they? Are they folks,
orders from some superior waves or are they engineered by alliances herein of
intergalactic entities, much like the wavefunction collapse we earlier mentioned being the
determined transformations of probabilistic subatomic 'elements' here dear folks in
a material world, not engineered by superior entities or waves or frequencies.
Our position is that both scenarios could be operational given our notions of
the continuum of consciousness of the immaterial and material herein laid yea.

They are essentially opposite faces of the same coin, in other words, un-embodied or
embodied waves or vibrations, so, our woes may be local or non-local which underscores the
point Foucault was making about power being everywhere, you know, even within us as persons
in our operations with friends, family, colleagues and all else, operating locally yea
albeit under the 'invisible' forces historicism says we lack control over,
our local power, as such, subject to some panopticon's oversight, the important point being
the exercise of power at different levels, any of which alone and in any of
a number of combination with other power levels and the roles these power structures and
operations play in the goings on in void we see at these various levels that baffle
us and create the 'mysteries' we say are abundant everywhere we look in void: mystic waves.

We seem to be so scared of these waves we are in some way participate in creating, but why?
The answer we may assume has something to do with those creepy forces over which we all lack
control but which, nonetheless control us, the hierarchy externalized in the structures laid out
over millennia to keep us all in check, the Leviathan that ruthlessly ensures we
are beggarly beggared to render us ineffective and much easier to control and yes
enslaved: these are the forces lined up against us that make us attack one another under some
so-called orders from above, along the hierarchical chain of command embedded here in void,
our tendency to be afraid of these forces perhaps due to not wanting to die, our fear of
death likely rooted in our understanding or lack thereof of what existence, more so as waves
is all about and whether or not there is an afterlife which, as we noted even fiends mull.

Having established that waves, regardless of their station in the hierarchy are all dear folks in
the intergalactic realm like the rest of us subject to the laws of nature to which we all
are be they of the classical or quantum physics form for example, as such, they are only
establishing bogus hegemonies here they label serfdoms, kingdoms or whatever-dom loading
us with fear making our lives permanently putting us in limbo yea, afraid of death, something
we may never know when it will come knocking on our doors no matter how afraid of it we are,
not to mention the chances of us misunderstanding what existence really is, more so in light
of us being mattered waves and by extension what death really means and whether or not we should be
afraid of it, in light of which we should bear in mind what the elder statesman we earlier said
about fear itself being the only thing we should fear, so, should we be afraid of death dear mates eh?

Folks, let us mull these things see if we should be afraid of death as it appears we currently are
that may explain why we so readily capitulate to the regime of snakes, viruses and
whatever else, creating a situation for ourselves that further dumbs us down herein since,
apparently, we are not supposed to read anything else but some prescribed sacred texts and some
dogmas, some 'little red book,' you know; a situation that also may not only ensure that
we remain slaves but also makes certain we don't even try to free ourselves from bondage fearing
the sanctions we face such as losing our sources of livelihood dreaming of no longer being slaves.
Could it be the case that all these would change if we better understood who and what we are and what
existence really is? Would we better comprehend death and be scared no more to die? Could we folks
then realize the bogusness of the hegemonies all around us perpetuated here?

Yes, we might be able to see the illusions in life perpetuated by people who want
us to continue to be their slaves, evil people who have cremated care and sold their souls to
Satan as some traditions have it and, talking about this entity our exploration yea
reminds us we are talking about an intergalactic wavefunction like the rest of us that
perhaps operates at the helm of an evil hierarchy of some very low frequency
waves capable of nothing but spreading bad vibes, evil miasmic waves, which ought to be truly
reassuring more so considering waves, including those low frequency demonic waves
operate along the continuum of consciousness and may or may not be embodied in
our material reality which should not demoralize us since, knowing what sorts of waves
are evil, we simply avoid them, we don't allow them any room in our lives, they are evil.

Whereas we embrace high frequency uplifting waves or frequencies or indeed music,
invite peace and love into our lives. This is a simple approach but our formulations suggest
it makes sense. We should not consider it a medical recommendation or treatment but as
heuristic, worthy of consideration as such, more so given the notion of us all being
waves herein in an intergalactic realm, including Satan who or what may, like all waves, be
miasmic or not depending on the nature and characteristics of the wave and yes its
alliances of embodied and disembodied waves. So, should we still be afraid of Satan, or folks
whatever wave herein engages in evilness in void understanding we are all waves and
alliances of waves more so understanding the prospects of waves being manifest in any
number of different forms, colors and sizes here in void O yes? Is fear of death really required?

We should be able to start seeing existence differently given the implications of
wavefunction collapse we are inferring here for our current notions of what existence really
means and, by extension, what death really means and, by further extension, what freedom really means.
We may spend the rest of the year talking about the ills of society, the oppression of
the masses by a few, the effects of climate change and the viral pandemic ravaging the
world but nothing will change, or not much will change O yes not mulling their root causes herein within
manifestations of waves and whatever else is involved in their material expressions
in a voided space, which should further reassure us that we have at least an inkling into what
and who might be responsible for wanting to erase 'today,' a realization that may
help us spring into action regarding breaking free of the fangs of snakes, setting ourselves free, yea.

Indeed, folks, better understanding waves may also help us see why we should not sit on the fence
playing ostrich while our world and us slide down the rabbit hole of darkness into the belly of

the beast as some traditions have it. We earlier noted that some of the deadliest fiends that
ever lived in our world appear concerned about where they head after death, do they know something we
don't? Do they know there is an afterlife of various kinds, for example heaven and hell? We
may not know for certain if they did or what their preferences among the examples we just
gave might be but that they are concerned about such things suggests they probably are aware that being
physically dead here in void is not the end of our peregrinations in the realm, which is
instructive and may prompt us to start thinking similarly and choosing between going yea to
a better or worse place after death, including taking steps that will enable us reach our goal.

So, folks, that we have much to gain adopting the wave approach to figuring out goings on in
our void, its eclectic approach to knowledge acquisition an eye-opener in many ways that
frees us from the cognitive constraints grand narratives impose on us, a deliberate device,
it appears by waves determined to keep us chained down in Platonic caves, to keep us uninformed
about ourselves and our world so we are uninspired to seek freedom from the perpetual jail
of slavery they have us and, as some traditions contend, that we may not become gods like them,
you know, wave-gods. We must reject such attempts to keep enslaving us forthwith, and we know they will
come after us but they can't kill us all, and they know we know about death, they know we know about
Elizabeth Frye and that we will not be in the grave, they know their time is up and the forces of
light will prevail over those of darkness, they know it's time for humanity to be free, at last.

Book 6

It is, indeed time for all of us to be free to choose where we want to head after our journey
in void ends, and we don't have to seek too far to realize we engage in evilness at our
own peril, that is if we did not consider going to an equally evil place a good
thing and did not think that evil doers go to good places and good doers yea go to evil
places after death, an inversion commonplace in today's world, so folks, it is reasonable
to want to do good if we cared about going somewhere good in the afterlife and vice versa:
there is no chicaning to Eden's gate! You have probably noticed that we have left out here the
notions of heaven and hell, this is because we do not want to create the impression you must
subscribe to any tradition to see why you must embrace goodness and eschew evilness as
the case may be, it's simply commonsensical to opt for goodness rather than evilness yea.

We say this not only because it is our choice but also that it would likely be your choice too
if you cared about going to good places after death and vice versa. So, we have also left
the decision-making in everyone's hands, after all, each person is answerable for their
actions here and as proclaimed by Hermes 'as above so below,' wherever we head after death
as well. It is our responsibility to pursue happiness not hurting others in the
process, but we don't see how sacrificing a child to some god or whatever, whilst pursuing
happiness could be deemed as not hurting others and a good deed, not at all, which is why we have
been calling out all manner of evilness going on in our precious world, things that may explain
the stance of some waves on whether or not we should forget about today, the here and now across
which they straddle to connect equally non-existent yesterday and tomorrow, in their heads.

As far they are concerned, today stands alone, essentially justifying forgetting it
as it has no viable link with any other day other than itself, a stance we hold may
have to do with a commitment to evil, certainly not to goodness, their position dear folks
suggestive of the pursuit of death rather than life and, as such, untenable to us, a view
we unreservedly reject and will continuously prevent O yes. So, dear folks, that we have decomposed
peoples and events in the void into quantum states has helped us see how whoever herein or
indeed elsewhere that might be tweaking our world are nothing other than waves morphing into matter
including into humans, plants, animals and anything in between with a wide range of intentions and agenda
some of may be good and others evil, the latter of major concern based on their potential to destroy our
lives, our civilization normalizing evil and to render our world extinct, outcomes, void.

We reject those outcomes outright and seek a brighter future for ourselves and our world, and will not
let those waves that do not wish us well achieve their malevolent goals, why we are advocates of
goodness and not evilness and urge folks to consider the former as the way forward yea for
ourselves our children and grandchildren and indeed all those coming after us. We have a lovely
world tailor-made for us with celestial bodies twinkling in the sky serenading music
of the spheres, which ought to inspire saltation in our hips or our shoulders not drones, folks not bombs to
babies kill not dynamites to farmers maim, we have a wonderful world to nurture and hoist its
flag aloft to elevate its face in the realms not smash it with fly-agaric rain, we have yea
a world we all ought to cherish not perish with global warming climate change dismissing just for
rice and some razzmatazz going down the gullets of ghouls striking demonic deals in coves in woods.

Yes, we can do more to save our precious world, we can choose to invest in clean energy fossil
fuels no more engage, we can do better than forging alliances deep in satanic woods
to hurt the environment, including the woods wherein we strike our evil deals, we can yes give
women equal pay for the same work as men we can give women the chance to have control over
their bodies and don't force them to have babies for rapists, adding insult to their emotional
injuries they did not ask for instead of being empathetic and supportive towards them, we
can save children from being infected with a terrible virus and dying of the disease it
causes by allowing them to wear face masks in school and getting vaccinated to prevent them
from catching the virus in the first place and we can stop passing legislation yea to suppress
voters we can stop destroying democracy we can do all these things and make our world much better.

One is wont to ask questions not for the fun of it but to find answers to the bizarreness we
see all around us such as those mentioned above, yet the more questions we ask the fewer answers
we find we could consider at least closer to the truth than most other answers, why is that? We
may need to dig deep into history to do better with the answers, after all many of
the bizarreness are not exactly new, what may be new folks is the brazenness with which they are
perpetrated with small and big lies, with misinformation and information asymmetry
and with the meddling of foreign countries in the elections of other sovereign states, some of these
activities so blatant it is incredible, more so as they appear to go unchallenged,
well, as some may say, it is what it is what are you going to do about it? We are going to refuse the
seeming normalization of evil and act to correct these anomalies at the polls, yes.

Right folks? Right! As we have been saying we are seeing a tendency for inversion to be the
order of the day, with evil been termed good and good, evil, without folks challenging it and, in
some cases, even embracing it! To be sure, we do not expect everyone to be of the
same religious or political persuasion, but as we earlier mentioned folks, to call
cremating care or sacrificing children to please some god a good thing as allegedly done
in some cultures ancient and modern a good thing is unlikely to be acceptable to most
people worldwide regardless of creed or dogma O yea, which makes this creepy tendency toward
normalizing evil quite concerning, a trend we must arrest yes folks we must all save ourselves,
protect our civilization and defend our very precious world yes we must folks, it is the
only world we have, one customized for us in atavistic waves upon which we must build progress.

We need to build progressive, not retrogressive waves on the atavistic epigenetic
epiphenomena we all are, we must not allow waves that care nothing about us other
than enslaving us to establish hegemonies in void and we must neutralize those they have
already established at the polls. We want to be hopeful of progress not be dejected and
lack it, we must operate in waves that spread good and not bad vibes, we must inject peace, joy and love
into our lives and work together to make our world a better place for all and sundry O yes,
there is nothing stopping us from doing these things but ourselves getting stuck in the mud of rice and
razzmatazz, succumbing to the temptation to sign up with demonic waves for a piece of the
evil pie we have been conditioned as sine qua non to the successful pursuit of joy yea,
whereas we know cash does not always bring happiness and it's surely not the only thing that does.

We do not have anything against money or anyone seeing it as the means to peace and joy
and to achieving whatever else they seek in life, but we are concerned about its corrupting

role in our democracy yes, more so in the electoral process, the key dear mates to the
emancipation of the masses we intend to accomplish, why we want to reinforce what
our notion of waves has taught us regarding the non-invincibility of our foes who are
nothing other than intergalactic waves like us although, unlike us, they are engaged yea in
shenanigans to corner our world and establish their evil rule over us, an agenda
we must all reject and deny these evil forces the chance to realize blocking them with our
votes, that they don't have to achieve their agenda is evident in the polls all over the world
as folks demonstrate their own 'hegemonies' at the ballot box: we believe in democracy!

We need to strengthen this belief and not allow any god or whatever to take it away
from us, we must protect and defend our fundamental rights as human beings no matter where we
live: it is imperative we do, the pursuit of freedom is a legitimate enterprise
we must not trivialize, more so aware of the plot of some people in our midst to enslave
us for aye, something some of them perhaps consider their god-given right, maybe unwary we
know a thing or two about waves, about music of the spheres, maybe they do not realize we
can dance not only with our hips but also with our shoulders O yes and, most of all, maybe they
do not realize the tide of history is against them and that no matter how many of
us they starve to death they are fried, they are on their way out and time is fast running out for them yea:
it is a brand new day the future ever bright, fear not, apotropaic forces on our side.

Book 7

We have nothing to fear folks, nothing at all, but fear itself: we have a lot to gain, our freedom most of all, something our conceptualizations have made us better understand, it's real value clearer in our minds, more so as we are better able to tell the difference between good and evil and to see our 'nakedness' or is it foolishness they mean, in a grove, something some waves don't want us to see, why they don't want us to wolf a pome, so that we don't become gods like them, so that we remain in the darkness of Platonic caves chained chasing shadows yea, being their slaves always, forevermore dear mates, why they would starve some of us to death for savouring that apple yes for daring to expose their smelly butts, even worse, for revealing their lies about being gods, some so-called potent ones who are nothing but slaves conspiring in demonic coves to lord it over us: they are intergalactic waves of the worst kind folks, pure evil creating chaos in our world.

Yes, fomenting trouble everywhere morphing into viruses, snakes and ravens and owls and yes, shimmering amorphousnesses and walking sticks, yes vectors, to confuse and intimidate us preaching one thing during the day and worshipping something else in the dead of night we are sick of these lunatics and their retarded antics and must end their evil regimes in our voided space before they render our precious world extinct. We no longer buy their fake smiles, the nasty lies they tweet. We know they don't tax the ballyhooed rich whose so-called wealth fund their campaigns verily here in void yet tax the poor to death, make us all unable to pay our medical bills and yes die poorer and bankrupt, yet their friends prey on us with psychedelic drugs peddled as anaesthetic and antidepressants, yes they pump hallucinogens into our heads, perhaps to get us all crazy, needing 'psychological tests' like they do, but they smile all the way to the bank, we don't.

Folks, what sort of a world is that and who or what is behind it? Well, that is the question yea our notion of waves is giving us an inkling into, telling us they are all manner of mattered entities that have something in common, namely, low frequency vibrations that spread bad vibes, what we refer to as miasmic waves, furthermore, and this is a crucial part, they all dear mates operate in the intergalactic realm wherein we are and operate, whether or not they are embodied, yes they are intergalactic waves that manifest immaterially or materially here in void, trying to bamboozle us into thinking and believing they are gods with some superior attributes that qualify them to be worshipped by us, you know, including incinerating our children to please them. Bull! Yet, they have been able to recruit some unscrupulous fellows among us to propagate even enforce these myths in their texts, yea.

O yes, in meta this and meta that they think in their evil minds we'll never be able to figure, but they have found out there is no hiding place for fiends, we will ferret them from their tents in the woods and they know it, they know truth is coming for lies to neutralize them, they know their lies, big or small are no longer winning hearts and minds but losing them, and fast. One cannot but wonder how these retards could think they will get away with their silly games in this day and age, yes really, how anyone could think that by doing a photo op with a bunch of guys and brandishing sky high a sacred text in front of a temple will make people vote for them! Doesn't that show how very retarded they truly are and how lowly they see us all? Lord have mercy! Okay, let them keep at it, let them continue to see and treat us like trash, they will soon find out whose is the trash when we vote them out regardless of their lobbyists, all their gerrymandering crab: just wait, they'll see.

Verily they will: they'll see the power we wield in action at the ballot box. Indeed, and we have already started seeing divisions among the perpetrators of the heinous crimes yea against humanity we have been talking about, we have started hearing people like the chief executive officer of large pharmaceutical companies expressing concerns about the pricing of drugs, we have started hearing concerns from an erstwhile treasury secretary about the tax cuts given the rich even in a left-leaning government, and we have started seeing rich countries agreeing to tax the rich to some extent. These are signs of changing times folks, if not of empty talk, considering we have heard these rhetorics before, well maybe they mean business this time, maybe they have started to see the writings on the wall after all, maybe they have realized we mean business and are trying to clean their stables who knows, dear mates eh?

Whatever be the case, we are not joking around, we want change and demand it, we will effect it at the polls sooner than later, so mote it be, we all now know how these folks hide a piece of chicken nugget in their mouths and declare it missing, we know how they bare their rotten teeth yes in a nasty grin, and we know how they make promises they toss once in office, we know all these things and are waiting for them at the polls, we are no longer playing the fool we are all now going nimble, we are getting smarter by the day analyzing void using our notion of waves, and that's what we need to do, we are tossing negativity and it's perpetrators and we are embracing positivity herein, aware that some of our folks are too far gone in their lives in captivity to see the void as waves but we will never give up on them, we will dear folks continue to persuade them to seek and receive the light, illuminated in darkened voids.

For sure, they could still hold on to aspects of their credos that don't interfere in any way with their abilities to seek and receive the light, aspects of their beliefs that don't turn them into zombies ordered around by some deranged leader to behead other people simply because they hold a slightly different version of essentially the same doctrine. These, folks are the sorts of situations some of our folks currently find themselves, their every move being monitored by those eyes, panopticons within their groups and social circles, to ensure they don't stray away from the doctrine: some of our folks are trapped in these sorry states, unable to leave lest be sanctioned by the groups, instructed by the leader we must all help them see the lies that have tied them down, lies those who try to debunk are labeled heretics and ostracized by the groups, we need to expose these demonic tactics of social control that have been used through the ages to keep us all enslaved.

We don't want to be slaves anymore we want to be free as the birds explore the realms be happy as a lad we want to chorus music of the spheres with the angels with the canaries yes the nightingales dance and sing our song in paradise with goodness in the air sung not evil on our lips, we want to be free, yes folks free to live our lives the way we want troubling no one but rather spreading goodness, joy and peace with goodwill in our hearts to everyone and everything yea in realms wherever they are dear mates, we really want to be free, we want to break free of the fangs of an ouroboros not end up recycled in the belly of an anaconda spat out in some consciousness much worse than we left, yes for evilness will beget its ilk in an even worse state and we don't want to be a part of that we want to embrace goodness to have a chance herein to enter Eden's gate, a place of perfected perfection folks able at last to yoke with ane, yea.

This is what we want to do and are prepared to work hard to achieve, why we must work with our kin, with our sisters and brethren and not try to leave them behind, we are all in this together and

only collectively do we stand a chance to stop these bugs from overrunning us and our world,
a chance we cannot afford to pass up one we must grab with zeal, folks we must not settle for less
than becoming free we must do all we can to ensure we are no longer taken for a ride
by a cabal of lizards and snakes and cats and whatever herein in our midst, we might as well
settle for the modernism reflected in the Victorian ethos of Rudyard Kipling's
'If,' and forever be aporetic and enjoy slavedom the best we can, right? It's an option,
or is it? Folks, we need to take these issues seriously we need to see the difference yea
between rice and razzmatazz and genuine spiritual freedom as some traditions say.

We must pursue genuine not flimsy 'happiness' that evil grants and at very high costs, indeed
folks, we must reject it regardless of the cost. Our foes will do anything to entice us and
will offer us the world to bow down at their feet and serve them O yes, for they need their supply of
sacrificial lambs they need gore, whatever form of energy they claim they need yes, they will not
kill us all they need the fresh energy that keeps the beast alive, and folks we are all workers in
their 'energy factories,' or so it seems, making babies at their behest how many and what
types, you know, what types of energy they really need, they specify, why they would castrate a slave
unable to get women pregnant or make the required number and types of babies, and why they
would stipulate the number of babies a family could have, you know, impose all sorts of things
on us, after all we are their slaves, Lord have mercy! Do we really want to live like this folks, eh?

Book 8

Why should we? Why should we forget Heraclitus who said, 'life is a child at play' and ignore the
irrational side of life Pythagoras and Lao-Tsu, all of whom lived in the same era
espoused, the side that science cannot explain and may not acknowledge despite its recognition
by the likes of Newton and Leibniz, the side of life we may need to start to pay attention to
that we may grasp what the Mystery schools tell us underlies the material reality
we share, what we are seeing perhaps an unprecedented 'escape' of evil waves yea from their
domain into our material world, a notion embodied dear mates in the continuum
of consciousness we have been talking about, these demons now roaming free in our void, as bugs yea
parasitizing on people creating chaos and confusion in our precious world dear mates,
a situation we must address, a trend we must reverse, pronto, that we may save ourselves yes.

There is no doubt that all is not well with our world, we cannot continue to be in denial
of the fact that we are going through a mysterious phase that seems difficult to comprehend
with many of us seemingly zombified taking marching orders to attack parliament
and kill people there, and many such bizarre things going on all around the globe have some people
opened the gates of hell and let the wolves out? What the heck is going on folks why are we being led
by our noses, goaded into the abyss as it seems, who is getting us all drunk on Lethe
straddling today they do not think exists anyway and just want us all to forget about it?
Who wants us to believe it does not exist just as the color white does not exist hence the need
for the white and black monk as some would contend, unwary of the illusion of the existence
of any color or anything at that, our reality as we have been saying, O yes.

Our views are consistent with the alchemical notion of the Matrix. 'conjured' herein out of
the interactiveness of waves resulting in a wavefunction collapse, in quantum mechanics
terms. In other words, there is a world behind our world we need to explore to understand goings
on in our world, the world of music of the spheres that begets our world whose music we need to be
able to sing and dance to that we may figure out our fleeting illusory reality,
a closely guarded secret for which Pythagoras lost his life when Cyron, a man he deemed too
rash to be admitted into his Mystery school, roused a group of people into a jealous
rage who set fire to the school killing all therein, so, folks, we have no time to waste addressing the
issues we face in our voided space, we must drive whatever demons terrorizing void back past
the blind between the material rational and the immaterial irrational world.

We must reclaim our reality, our world, O yes, we cannot and must not sit back and let some
demon masquerading as viruses and people 'rule' our world, we should never do that, we have
no better chance of an opportunity to follow in the footsteps of Pythagoras yea
regarding working together to achieve a common goal, the rudiments of democracy
that helped the Delian League, an alliance of Athens and hundreds of Greek city-states formed
in 478 B.C consolidate Greek victory over the Persians in
the Battle of Plataea which ended the Second Persian invasion of Greece, which Sparta helped
with, between 480 B.C and 479 B.C O yes,
we need to build on the democratic principles born in Athens in those days and join hands to
defeat the virus plaguing our void regardless of its source, we must face our challenges unfazed.

It is clear from the aforementioned that esoteric and exoteric knowledge exists, the
nature and veracity of both knowledge bases not always unquestionable given they
are prone to being value-laden and are plagued by charlatans dear mates, as such, in exploring and
seeking answers to the questions we raise concerning goings on in our world we all need to be
careful in interpreting the information we obtain, we need to careful adopting views
cooked up, redacted and curated to lead us astray for the selfish ends of some so-called scribes
or whoever put the information together, examples of such misinformation
commonplace today, organized by who or what we could term malevolent waves or entities
herein essentially normalizing these practices that result in the propagation of
bogus meta-narratives in some virtual space that reminds us of our irrational side.

Yes, folks, the irrational, immaterial side of life that its rational, material
side begets, so you see, we could inadvertently be entrenching demons here in our body
politic allowing this weird normalization being reckless in adopting big or small lies.
There is too much going on in our fast-changing world to adopt the ethos in 'If,' at least some
of it, particularly those aspects instructing us basically to be aporetic,
no we cannot be basically silent we must talk a lot about our issues and out loud,
we must holler atop the mountain top scream our pain to the realms we must complain and explain and
not just sit here and calculate, as some physicist once suggested, we must ask why the .1
percent of us who control the global wealth are getting tax cuts while the rest of us are getting
taxed like crazy herein in a void, we must want to know what makes these fellows so special herein.

What makes them so special they are treated like sacred cows while the rest of us are treated like their
dung? Some queries have ready answers others do not, this one, somewhere in between. On the one hand
we may view it with exoteric eyes, which limits us to things such as the influence of cash,
the power of lobbyists, the interplay of secret societies, and the power of threats
and coercion of all sorts among others, on the other hand dear folks we may view it yea with
esoteric eyes, which takes us behind the curtain of the alchemical Matrix to the world
of demons, the spirits of the dead and of gods in a bottom up hierarchy, according to
some Egyptian Mystery schools, so we are saying any of these immaterial waves yes
could be behind goings on in void, including giving the rich a special status and, indeed,
conferring wealth on them in the first place, hmm, what a revelation that would be if really true.

This is more so as it means these so-called rich people may be backed by both exoteric and yes
esoteric waves making it easier to see why they are so specially-treated, you know,
and no government seems courageous enough to tax them accordingly but rather folks they are
eager to give them tax cuts and create loopholes in the tax codes for them to pay almost nothing
if anything in taxes on their massive wealth: what sort of a world is that may we ask again?
Well, the answers to our questions may have suddenly become readymade, for in this case we could
say it's a world of women and men with stylish sun-glasses guarding the curtain of the Matrix:
yeah right, what are you talking about? I am talking about nothing, just the Matrix, you know, the
alchemical Matrix where our illusory reality is 'conjured' by transformative
changes in waves by wavefunction collapse, that's all! Okay, gotcha, I'm calling the cops, and a shrink!

Don't be surprised that these waves label us whimsy, at best and are ever ready yes to order
a psychological assessment to declare us insane, yet we wonder folks who really needs

chlorpromazine herein! The point about the difficulty talking about the irrational,
immaterial side of life more so in relation to it being the spring of the rational
material side of life is not hard to swallow especially if you were a scientist yes,
never mind some of the greatest scientific minds such as Isaac Newton might have spent more of
their time on finding the 'philosopher stone' than on his theory of infinitesimal
calculus. Seriously, are we surprised malevolent waves would not embrace goodness? We do
not expect them to embrace anything other than evilness and frankly, we do not care, we
care less they will do anything to try to silence us for we will not be silenced, we'll survive.

Let's not be afraid let us forge ahead towards our goal and, as evident, our explorations
and analyses are yielding results and giving us a clearer picture of what is really
happening in our world that its crooked operators don't want us to know, why folks we must not
falter and must be ever more determined to achieve our goal of saving ourselves and making
our world a better place for every one of us, a goal that we must hold sacrosanct and not let
any grand narrative derail: we are here right? We are operating in the exoteric
side of life even if we are aware of being in relation herein to esoteric side
of life and their cryptic operations, which might be what historicism refers to yes as
processes that control us but over which we lack control, O well, figure that out too, somehow,
our explorations will get us there, we will comprehend how our world works free ourselves at last, yes.

Book 9

No matter how long it takes, and we believe it will not take very long, we will eventually figure out our world, in full. It would be nice to know how these various esoteric and yes exoteric operations occur. We have speculated on energy exchanges in the immaterial esoteric side of what we term a continuum of consciousness whose results manifest on the material exoteric side. This is consistent with what the Mystery schools say about the source of our illusory reality, O yes folks, the reality we share, with its imbuing its vegetable state with animal life, in the case of humans, by a snake yea, more so in giving us the spine, so here we see the importance of action rather than form in our conceptualizations of void. Here we have seen the metaphor of the snake in very different ways, some good others bad, which tells us we must be careful to not get carried away by form.

We may have malevolent reptiles and we may have benevolent ones: folks we must remember reptiles even attack and devour one another in the wild! So, we are not going about looking for lizard eyes and cat eyes, but what they do here in our world, which underscores our focus on waves and their transformations into all manner of forms and indeed, their abilities to morph from form to form even in the same person who may, as such, have lizard eyes one minute and cat eyes or almond eyes the next, which highlights the fast-changing nature herein of the energy exchanges we earlier mentioned with shifting dominance of hegemonies and O yes in alliances making it difficult to pin down the particular wave behind goings on in our world, yet we are able to identify the evil things we see herein as being the handiworks of evil typically low-frequency waves and the good things those of good waves, yea.

Yes, we see the good things going on herein as the works of high-frequency waves, and the songs emanating from these waves as either ugly or sweet melodies to the human ear O yes, respectively, the latter music of the spheres folks like Pythagoras would hear, folks able to perceive both the esoteric and the exoteric sides of life, that is, an ability initiates of the Mystery schools aim to acquire, one we must all aim to acquire choosing the path of goodness and life and not the path of evilness and death, a choice we all have to make in our peregrines, one that is germane to the outcome of these journeys after we die, why we must pay close attention to our actions here while alive and ensure they are consistent with where we want to head when we expire here realizing what we have learned about us being waves and yes about the meaning of the freedom we seek, you know, realizing the need for us to have proper views.

We need to have the proper perspectives on existence that we may make the choices we really want to make, folks we cannot afford to remain in the darkness of Platonic caves folks chasing ephemeralities, no that is not helpful in achieving our aim, that will only keep us enslaved as our overlords intended yea, we need to keep in mind that these are metaphors for being unable to express our freedom to choose whether to also see the esoteric side of life, the true reality or only its exoteric side, it's illusory herein manifest in a voided space, so folks this is what the freedom we seek is all about O yes, it transcends the experience of slavery in material terms and posits freedom as being the emancipation of the individual to harness all of their potential to figure out what is really going on in our lives and in our voided space, what we seek to know.

This is an ability the forces of darkness and evil do not want us to have lest, as
they say we acquire the knowledge of good and evil and become gods like them, which ignites them to
come after us with gall when we attempt to break free of their chains in our jails in those horrible
caves, and why we should not be perturbed by their vicious persecution for we already have the
knowledge they are trying to stop us acquiring even contemplating breaking free of their chains,
for this means we already know they are evil waves no matter how many private jets they try
to bribe us with and we know the outcomes of evil waves is why we reject them and seek the light
of ane, eternal light that never dims O yea, infinity within our reach, yes, we do not need to be afraid for we
know the outcomes of good waves, outcomes no amount of persecution can change why we must stay the
course and be steadfast in our belief in the choice we made to tread the path of life, not that of death.

That's right, folks we must keep treading the path we believe determines where we want to head after our
journeys in this world ends and, as we earlier noted, we know physical death is not the end
of our wave, the atavistic epigenetic epiphenomena we are dear mates yes,
upon which accretions herein build creating continuous transformations until folks we
physically expire O yes, transformations the onus is on us to ensure do not at
all derail our choice of where we head after we expire, whether heaven or hell according to
some traditions or characterized in some other ways, so folks, we need to take this task very
seriously and act accordingly, engaging in good deeds that will make us more likely to
attain ascension and be in a better place rather than be recycled in the belly of
the beast to emerge in an even worse and more primitive reality than we were in, yea.

Indeed, some traditions remind us we may end up being back in a state worse than before we died,
having lost the little progress if any we made in our previous lives treading the path of
death doing evil deeds, so folks, it's our choice where we want to head and end, it is up to us to
choose but, thankfully, the knowledge we have acquired seeing reality as manifestations
of waves is likely to stand us in good stead as we set about taking this crucial step and yes
embarking on the next stage of our spiritual journeys in the realms, as we are now folks more
familiar with the esoteric and exoteric sides of life and realize evil
waves are behind all the evil things we see going on in void, evil ways people like you and
me operate, people we must therefore prevent from holding positions of authority that
they may no longer be able to stand in our way of taking the decision to do good deeds.

We must vote out and not vote in people who are engaged in actions detrimental to our goal
of breaking free of the shackles of slavery and making our world a better place for us, we
must see these people for who they truly are, evil waves lurking in our space and we must not let
them destroy us and render our world extinct. We must embrace persons who will create dear folks the
enabling milieu for us to tread the path of life we wish to tread. We should take actions on our
parts at the polls that are consistent with good deeds as we play our parts to attain the freedom we
seek and save our precious void. Remember folks, we are under attack by these evil waves, we have
been languishing in a pandemic now for quite a while, a pandemic a virus that's killing
many of us morphing into variants and sub-variants caused, our way of life altered our
economy shattered by these evil waves so they are not to be ignored, not at all dear mates.

Actually, we need to redouble our efforts to comprehend these waves at exoteric
and esoteric levels that we may be better able to protect ourselves and defend our

world. We need to see ourselves as being under siege by malevolent waves herein embodied and
disembodied in our precious world and be determined to squarely face the challenges they pose,
challenges we ought to see as existential threats in the context of our understanding of
the operations of waves O yes, threats that hinder our ability to tread the path of life,
threats that ask us to forget today exists and straddle yesterday and tomorrow that we are
all also supposed to believe do not exist just so they can justify their evil actions
and claim we need not see them as evil but actually as good since we are not encumbered
by the guilt of yesterday and the fear of the unknown, some warped logic to justify evil.

Is it some crazed justification for sacrificing tots to some lunatic gods? Sorry, we
are not sold! We prefer to see a future and to acknowledge yesterday, we prefer to see
both and today as processes inherent in our peregrinating we cannot wish away,
processes we want to modify for the progress of humanity in keeping with our choice
to tread the path of life and do good things while alive here in a voided space dear mates, that
we may surely achieve ascension and be admitted into the perfected perfection of
Eden yes, so folks, let us keep working hard to reach this goal let us not trivialize folks the
challenges we face and how the choice we make between doing good or evil may have damaging
and enduring implications for us and our world, why must all be engaged and play our parts in
ensuring a better and brighter future for everyone herein in our precious world O yes.

Book 10

This is our chance to make a difference change our world for better not for worse. We may or may not
choose to seize the opportunity of a lifetime in an age chaos reigns supreme everywhere
you look, our world rammed by a nasty virus morphing unrestrained, our lives in limbo entangled
in a viral web we struggle to exhale, Lord who did we roil queries every lip as folks young
and old succumb to Covid-19 glassy lungs our bane, so who will toss a chance to change this state,
who will refuse to face this evil wave? Your guess and mine align and it is not even one, the
situation crystal clear no need for any philosophical debate on what is good and
what is evil dear mates: only an evil wave will refuse to fight the virus being together
kin, O yes, both with evil gore running in their veins, both lacking empathy ready yea to send
millions of folks to an early death, so the die is cast we must engage a bug in a just war.

There is no looking back folks we must fight and win this war we must defeat the bugs menacing void.
Onward ever backward never folks must our mantra be, no matter the obstacles we may face
along the way, regardless of the plots and conspiracies of our foes to stop us: we must not
be fazed we must not be afraid knowing what we now know about the operations of waves on
the esoteric and exoteric sides of life, no folks we must strong remain assure ourselves
we will best the bug, yet we must not give up on exploring the inner workings of our world as
we know we have a lot more to learn about the music of the spheres the workings of the gods,
in particular we need to know much more about the evil waves doing a wicked number
on us in our voided space, we need to know what they really want and what we must do to rid our
void of bugs although we hold they'll naturally disappear once we keep voting them out of void.

That is precisely what we will continue to do as we learn more about these malicious waves.
We have speculated on why waves might be evil, including the need for a peculiar type
of energy fresh gore provides, an exoteric level consideration that may reflect
an esoteric level need, that is if we are not thinking that the high priests of the gods are
appropriating the sacrifices behind the scene, a notion which that of tophets yea
and possibly even that of the cremation of care may render questionable, so mates the
option remains, yet we must not assume it is the only one, we must explore others as it
is important for us to have an idea of what the evil waves really want to achieve
holding us hostage in Platonic caves, knowing which may go a long way in helping us win the
anti-virus war, a war we cannot afford to lose, and will not lose dear mates, so mote it be.

Whatever their motives are, it is obvious that they are evil and not dear folks in the best
interests of humanity. That a small number of people, who we should all herein assume
is representative of the internalized hierarchy of hegemonic waves, as is of
often said, the .1 percent of the world's population who control its wealth are up
to no good for the rest of the world and someone has to call them out, we cannot let these very
inane and unscrupulous elements continue to destroy a world that belongs to all of
us, we must trim their egos and bring them back to ground level from their joy rides in space and yes their
broomsticks: we, the masses say we've had enough, this nonsense must stop, we must have democracy
everywhere in void and we must elect those who want to save our world from the menace of bugs and
viruses, and all, not just their family and friends, and they need to hear us loud and clear, okay?

The world has enough resources equitable distributed to take care of everyone of
us but alas, these enemies of democracy don't want that, they want a fascist world wherein
they enslave the rest of us claiming some god-given right to lord it over us, or declaring
in public they are the 'chosen one' brandishing sacred scriptures taking photographs in front of
temples yea, retards! Imagine such nincompoops claiming to be authorized to press a button
and bomb the world out of existence! Lord have mercy. There is no gainsaying the fact that the world
is tethered on a cliff, precariously, threatened with being 'unleashed' if it didn't dance, not to
the sonorous music of the spheres but to the roiling music of the squares, or whatever! Yes,
democracy is under siege in the hands of the emissaries of Satan, and their army
of demons and the spirits of the dead who were in their ranks while alive and of their evil gods.

Yes, let's go to the Egyptian Mystery schools, folks let's listen to the warnings of an ibis
from the past see the plight of Oxymandias as child's play compared to what we face yea dear mates
following the orders of our foes to forget today, let us listen to the dinosaurs who
are 'begging' us from their graves to learn a thing or two from their fate let us folks do something about
climate change, about pervasive poverty worldwide let us do something to save democracy
yea, let us do something to break free of the fangs of snakes, yes let us seek freedom and be free for
freedom is sine qua non to democracy, securing our fundamental human right to
be free is the first crucial step towards ensuring democracy survives and folks we must all
ensure it does lest we are back in an Hobbesian state we thought we left behind long ago,
yes, we are back in the 'dog eat man' state not even our so-called rulers want to contemplate, yea.

So, they have a stake in saving democracy too, whether or not this registers in their thick,
fat, empty skulls, we all have a stake in turning our backs against the demons and whatever who
seem to have a stranglehold on us at the moment forcing us to worship them, threatening us
and our families with harm if we didn't, setting up demonic social and other networks
of panopticons to keep us all in line and viciously going after some of us who yes
flatly reject their hegemonies trying their darnedest to destroy us: this is the 'dark ages'
in the C21st tophet-monsters perpetuate! Bull! We will meet them at the polls!
This is our story, our song, our faith our hope for humanity, we must not fail folks we must stay
the course we must win the war against the parasites that have invaded the world and win the hearts
and minds of folks that we may stop their agents from ever taking control of our precious world.

We must stop them at the polls and not by any violent means: our democratic will is sure
enough to stop these evil agents of Satan who they call their 'boss' taking over our world and
we will, we will stop them in their tracks and drive their demonic principals yes back into the deep
abyss where they belong, they don't belong here, they belong in hell! They are parasites and only
live and thrive feeding off us, they are leeches folks, demonic leeches we must shake off our void, O
yes, we are not going to be fodder for bugs we will not be dinner for snakes we will not be
slaves to anyone knight or knave, we are not going to cry no more we are going to smile and
be happy we are going to emancipate ourselves and save our world, we are going to win
the war against these evil waves at the polls and we cannot gainsay that folks, we cannot at all
overstate the need for us to defend and save democracy if necessary with our lives.

Remember what we have been saying about existence about waves? Yes, we are waves and we do
not sleep as Elizabeth Frye reminds us, there is acacia on our graves, so mote it be! Let's

make it happen folks, let's kick these assholes, pardon my language, out of our lives and our world O yes!
We can do it mates and we must, we must free ourselves from slavery, preserve democracy and
save our precious world, this is not an ego trip, it is a fight for survival and we are all
at risk of being sucked dry of gore by demons, yes this is their motive we have been searching for: these
brutes are parasites and like every other parasite, live and thrive feeding off others, sucking them
dry and moving on to other preys, so we are being preyed on for their survival yes at our own
expense, we are their 'baby factories' that must be in operation all the time, sustained folks
with the active participation of their externalized hierarchies all over the world, yes.

Yes, folks, these demons have entrenched themselves and infiltrated every sphere of our lives, in art, in
religion, politics, academia you name it, even in our families, their evil
satanic networks miasmic in a void, but we will not be deterred, folks we will continue
exposing these brutes unfazed, no matter how much they persecute us regardless of their tricks and
pranks and the games they play to confuse us and instil fear in us: we are not afraid of them and
will fight them tooth and nail at the polls, we will fight and defeat the bugs and viruses folks, for sure
we will, so, let's go out there and vote, all of us young and old, go folks, go vote them leeches out and
never vote them in, success will be ours so mote it be. We are many we are strong we will vote
in every election and even stronger be. We will not worship Satan or whatever we
will no longer be slaves to anyone or anything we are free for eternity, O yea.

www.ingramcontent.com/pod-product-compliance
Lightning Source LLC
Chambersburg PA
CBHW060929130726
48001CB00006B/2491